Poems
from
Homeroom

Kathi Appelt

Poems from Homeroom

A WRITER'S PLACE TO START

Henry Holt and Company
New York

While most of the poems in this collection were written in the solitude of my studio, none were completed without the careful reading and commentary of several of my closest associates. For their honesty and openness, I'm indebted to Debbie Leland, Donna Cooner, Diane Linn, Deena Hardin, and Elizabeth Neeld. My mom, Pat Childress, and my sisters, B. J. Yewens and Patti Miller, made sure that I didn't forget to find some humor along the way. My sons, Jacob and Cooper, kept me grounded throughout. Stephen Shearer, a fellow poet, is a genius when it comes to inspiring kids to write—thank you for using my poetry in your classroom. My agent, Marilyn Marlow, always my guiding angel, provided constant encouragement, as did her associate, Elizabeth Harding, and her assistant, Brandon VanOver—also angels. To Kate Farrell, my editor, thank you for asking the hard questions and for making it feel easy at the same time. And finally, for my husband, Ken, I'm amazed by love.

Henry Holt and Company, LLC
Publishers since 1866
175 Fifth Avenue
New York, New York 10010
www.HenryHoltKids.com

Henry Holt® is a registered trademark of Henry Holt and Company, LLC.
Copyright © 2002 by Kathi Appelt
All rights reserved.
Distributed in Canada by H. B. Fenn and Company Ltd.

Library of Congress Cataloging-in-Publication Data
Appelt, Kathi.
Poems from homeroom : a writer's place to start / Kathi Appelt.
    p.   cm.
Summary: A collection of poems about the experiences of young people and a section with information about how each poem was written to enable readers to create their own original poems.
1. Teenagers—Poetry. 2. High school students—Poetry. 3. Young adult poetry, American. 4. Poetry—Authorship. [1. Teenagers—Poetry. 2. American poetry. 3. Poetry—Authorship.]   I. Title.
PS3551.P5578 P64 2002   811'.54—dc21   2002067886

ISBN- 9780805075960
First Edition—2002
Printed in the United States of America on acid-free paper. ∞

P1

To Cooper and Brian,
because you have a lot to say
and you say it so well
Love, K. A.

Contents

Poetry Is the Home for All My Yearnings

What is it that we yearn for? What is it that calls us to put a pen to paper? A brush to the canvas? A note to a song? What are the things that move us to act?

Since the very beginnings of the human race, we've been gathering in circles and telling stories because, beyond the physical needs for food, water, clean air, and security, one of our most basic yearnings is to express ourselves. This desire for expression may show up in dance, in art, in music, in our clothing, in the myriad ways in which we pierce our bodies; it even shows up in the friends we choose, for our associations say something about us too.

One way or another, if we have something to say, we're going to say it.

The thing is, ever since someone figured out that blood from an animal or dye from a plant leaves a visible mark on a piece of skin or a cave wall, one of the most available forms of expression has been writing.

And the great thing about writing is that it appears in a huge variety of forms. One of the most flexible is poetry. Poetry can be about the most mundane and inconsequential things—my father's cigarettes, a favorite coffee cup, a pair of shoes—or it can be about *big* things like war, terrorism, AIDS, and God. I've written about all of those.

However, aside from "Homeroom," I chose to write each of the poems in this collection about a person, someone I've met up close and personal, someone I've read or heard about, or in some cases, someone I just dreamed up. One of the great things about writing is the freedom you have to make up people, places (such as my fictional town of Dogwood, Texas), and times (the realm of science fiction writers!). This latitude gives you a sense of power, for sure.

When we create a character, the essential thing we must figure out is what motivates that character, what drives that person to do whatever it is he or she chooses to do. In other words, what is the spark behind the motion? What makes the character fly off the cliff or retreat into the backyard?

The answer is not always clear. Sometimes a character is driven by more than one thing. So the writer must ask: What does the character long for? What does he or she yearn for more than anything else? At the same time, you have to keep in the back of your mind what the *writer* is yearning for. For example, in "Seven Elegies to Those We Lost Too Soon," my motivation was to honor those young artists by taking a look at their lives rather than their deaths.

Sometimes it's easy to say that the character longs for a car or a date to the prom. But I've tried to sidestep the easy answers and am asking you to go along with me on the more complex longings that all of us experience at one time or another as we meander through life.

For the most part, the poems in this collection are about teenagers or young adults, people who are right at the cusp of taking charge of their lives, and in some cases already have. At no other time do we experience yearnings with such passion or power.

Poetry gives us a way to dip into our own motivations, as well as create other characters and dip into theirs. The purpose of Part Two of this book is to invite you to use my poems as "beginnings."

To help you enter the poems, I've given you a little background information about each one, why I came to write it, what inspired me, and who the poems might be about. Then I've identified the particular longing that I felt motivated the characters.

Warning: Keep in mind that sometimes we don't discover the motivation until after the poem is written, so don't let the motivation trap you. You may set out to write about someone who wants to run away and end up with a character who decides that home is the best place after all.

One thing you'll notice is that many longings are contradictory. For instance, at any given time in our lives, we may long for attention and then later wish we were invisible. Likewise, we have moments we'd like to forget and others we want to remember. These contradictions are what make life so extraordinary.

In addition, with each poem I've brainstormed a list of ideas for writing your poems. Keep in mind that the ideas are simply places to start. As I said, I often use the poetry of other writers to inspire my work. If one of my poems—or a poem from another poet—inspires you to write, then the tradition of poetry will continue.

I once heard that all great artists are also great imitators . . . the rest are just mediocre. The same can be said of writers. I'm a shameless imitator. When writing my sestina, "The Research Paper," I read several sestinas by other poets. In my opinion, Elizabeth Bishop should be crowned queen of this complex form for her wonderful poem called simply "Sestina." Just as I used her work as a model for mine, and just as Allen Ginsberg used the poetry of Walt Whitman as his, I'm hoping you'll use my poems to create yours.

So, grab a piece of paper and a pencil and go for it. At the very least you'll write a really, really bad poem. I write lots of those. In fact, I have whole notebooks and file drawers full of them. But chances are, if you keep at it, you'll eventually write a really, really great one too.

PART ONE

Homeroom: The Poems

Homeroom

Poetry is the home for all my yearnings
each poem a separate room
where wandering words
find a cool bed, a bowl of soup

where names of trees and cities
and people I know who want to know
knock on doors, ring bells,
invite me in for coffee and a rhyme

where a loose tooth
and a caladium can meet
in the same stanza
share the same breath
split a doughnut on the sofa. . . .

Let me come home then, and
let me bring my lusting with me
and if you find a room
that fits, that pulls you
in and pushes you out
then call that a "homeroom"
hang your own pictures
on its invisible walls
(use juicy colors
that fill up your mouth like a sneeze—
crocodile green, periwinkle,
    saffron)
carve your own desires
on its invincible hearth.

Make a poem
build a home.

Lost in the Blues

Jimmy Haliburton had to leave
his real guitar at home
an old Ibanez his Uncle Jay
gave him two Christmases ago.

It lay across his unmade bed
waiting for him to return
and he would, his fingers
pressing the wire against
the smooth wood of the neck.

But for now he sat in the corner
of his classroom, alone with his other guitar
the one made of air
and played along in perfect rhythm to
the morning announcements—
    pep rally at four (B flat)
    Spanish Club (A minor)
    yearbook staff (key of C).

Next thing he knew he was off
fingers flying across the frets
notes wailing through the invisible strings
in a circle around his brain—

listen, the blues have soaked right in
to that boy's air guitar, his supple fingers,
his beating heart,
now he's Jimi Hendrix
pledging allegiance through the night
with stars all around.

Oh say, can't you see—
you can't mess up or play out of key
when your guitar's made of air
you can't play the blues all alone.

The Tattoo Dragon

Curled around her ankle
like a cat
blue red green
the arrow tip of its tail
rested between
her large toe and the tall man next to it
she called it her pet
its leathery wing covered her
anklebone like a boot
the fine-tipped fins of its back
cut across her Achilles tendon
just below the skin
and disappeared beneath her heel
puffs of blue smoke billowed
from its narrow jaws
toward her knee like diamonds
green scales red scales
shimmered when she walked

what it came to:
she was no longer just
plain ol' Patty Lopez
one more face among the many no no
now she was Dragon Girl of Dogwood High—
fire-breather

Good Job, Buddy

Food City, 2 A.M., he tucks in his
red and black uniform shirt as
he passes the paperback books
where he knows she'll arrive soon.
All the masters of mystery are there:
    Mary Higgins Clark,
    Clive Cussler,
    Richard North Patterson,
    Dean Koontz most of all.
He hurries by, tonight's the night, he knows it . . .
he loves to work this shift,
the fluorescent lights humming,
a steady thrum just behind his ears.

He and the other boys load cases of Ragú and
Hamburger Helper onto carts,
roll them down the aisles,
there they slice the cardboard,
a jagged swish of utility knives.
He loves the danger of it, the pull of the blade toward
his thigh, knowing a slip could sever
his thumb or his first finger, could slice
through his black denim pants, the
ones he wears every night, required.
It's a dance he does with the
razor blade and boxes

a-one, a-two, a-three . . .

would Lacey dance if he asked?
He glances at paperbacks—
too early, Dean Koontz, he thinks.

He places the jars and bottles in quick
rows on the shelves, labels facing out like flags—
    the Republic of Kraft, the United Emirates
    of Nabisco, the Duchy of Birds Eye,
    the kingdom of discounts and coupons and
    a greeting card for every occasion.
Oh, would she dance if he asked?
The young night manager, Roy, turns
off the subliminal music—Neil Sedaka,
Marvin Gaye, Barry Manilow—Mandy oh Mandy—
and pipes in the local rock station, KRUD,
heavy metal washes down the aisles in waves of
drums and electricity, it races up his feet, through the
bones in his legs, pumps the blood right through his
    chest.
"Yeehaw," he wants to scream. "Yeehaw!" he screams.
He loves heavy metal, its driving pulse.

Soon he finds his own subliminal rhythm,
he's got the beat . . . canned tomatoes fly
onto the metal shelves, Campbell's Cream of Mushroom
settles neatly next to Split Pea, boxes of Jell-O—
raspberry, cranberry, lemon—line up like soldiers
waiting for inspection. He stands back and salutes.
Who could have dreamed he'd get such satisfaction
    out of
rows of instant gelatin? Who could have dreamed
he'd dream so much about her . . . Lacey.

Roy pats him on the shoulder. "Good job, buddy,"
he shouts over the grinding music. Good job, he thinks
as he glances at his watch—3:30. She should be here
    soon.
His steps are full of little hops he can't stop himself from
    taking.

Good job, he thinks as he sings along
with Jack from produce up to his knees
in cantaloupes fresh from the Valley,
sweet and round and juicy.
Ahh . . . cantaloupes . . . ahh . . .
Lacey!

Good job, he thinks, as he walks to cereal, Aisle 14,
his favorite—and no wonder—all his childhood friends
    are there
    Tony,
    Snap, Crackle, and Pop,
    Count Chocula,
    Fred and Barney . . .
but she, she should be here soon,
he looks at Cap'n Crunch—why didn't you
warn me, he asks? Then lines up the Trix and Kix
and Cocoa Puffs, Froot Loops, Cheerios, and Total . . .
he's almost to the end of the aisle, somewhere
between Post and General Mills, near the
check-out counter, he turns the corner,

smack! She's there! Lacey,
parked in the paperback books
just like he knew she would be
4 A.M., like clockwork, like an alarm
his heart skips at least three beats,
he finishes with the Raisin Bran.

Almost every night, after her shift at the Pancake
    House,
still wearing her blue apron and plastic Lacey name tag,
she floats into Food City, blond hair
tied back, back, back Lacey.

He holds a box of Grape-Nuts against his chest and
     watches . . .
each night she reaches behind the stack of
mysteries, and pulls out the newest Dean Koontz
. . . no one asks her to pay for it. What is it about
Dean Koontz?

Once, after she left, he hurried to paperbacks and
pulled out the copy she had so recently held.
He brought it to his face and breathed
in the scent of her—pancakes, strawberries,
and something else . . . a mystery.
The music bounced along the linoleum
filled the bags of miniature marshmallows
and frozen shrimp, filled his nostrils,
his eardrums, his fingers with resonance
so deep he couldn't name it.
Would she dance with Dean Koontz?
He knew she would.
But what did Dean Koontz know about her
quiet manner, her punctuality, her small frame,
the smell of syrup?
He sighed. Metallica rolled toward
him from the loudspeaker. All at once he
hated Metallica, its ear-splitting wall of noise.
There she was with her mysteries
all alone, and here he was alone with only Grape-Nuts
tight against his chest. And what he wanted
was his mother's old Simon and Garfunkel albums,
something soft, like Lacey.

Suddenly, he knew he had to
get her attention . . . had to make her see him
had to had to had to . . . that's when
all reason, all intelligence, all hope of
ever being considered normal again

left his body, walked right out through his skin
stranded him in cereal, where he set the Grape-Nuts
down in the middle of Fruity Pebbles and

without a thought grabbed an empty shopping cart,
a wide-nosed bundle of stainless steel,
and began to run.

Up and down the rows he went,
past the bins of onions and Irish potatoes,
the yellow squash and broccoli heads,
past Orville Redenbacher and Sun-Maid Raisins,
down the rows of canned vegetables,
earlyspringpeas-artichokehearts-limabeans-navybeans
greatnorthernbeans-creamedstylecorn-hominy
the colors flew by in a rainbow beside his vision
faster he went, then faster and faster,
the basket hummed in front of him. He saw the
rice and pasta, the rows of spaghetti sauce—
Mama mia, holy Toledo, shazam!
He's almost there, only frozen foods between
them, Stouffer's, Borden, Pepperidge Farm,
faster, faster, he pushes, he pushes, then all at once
the cart is pulling, pulling, pulling . . .
he's hanging on with all his might.

The cart has taken over. It pulls him past meat
and cheese, past paper goods, past pet food,
past the young night manager Roy.

Finally, the magazines! And just past that—
the paperbacks—romances, adventures, comics,
how-tos, bestsellers, Lacey!

His stomach cramps, his legs drag.
He can do this. He knows he can. He must do this.

Then, just as he nears the turn, he leaps . . .

the air rushes beneath him, his body flies above
the green and white linoleum, he pulls himself forward
both feet are on the bottom bar now,
his palms sweat, he's breathing hard, he takes a gulp,
with a mighty heave he jerks the cart toward him

did he do it? could he do it? is he flying?
Yes!

Victory! He and the cart are one
balanced on its two back wheels, a wheelie to end
all wheelies! There's never been another like it
in the history of Food City. "Yeehaw," he wants to
    scream.
"Yeehaw!" he screams. He sails past her
and lets go with one hand, which he raises to her,
lets go of his heart, which he throws her way,
lets go of his senses, which he left back there in
    cereal . . .
Kaboom, splat, errrrrrrrt . . . he crashes into Dr Pepper.

Is there a doctor in the house?

What in the world possessed him?
Keebler Elves? The Jolly Green Giant?
Oscar Mayer, the great weiner himself?

He's pretty sure he'll never again hear Roy
say, "Good job, buddy." He's certain
he's bruised his ribs. He knows for sure
that he's going to pay for all that Dr Pepper.

But like a voice from heaven . . .
"Are you okay?"

He doesn't think he is . . .
he's sure he's not . . .
maybe he'll walk again . . .
oh, what difference does it make?
All he can see is her blue apron,
her plastic Lacey nametag,
she fills the aisle with the scent of maple
looking down at him, so soft, and. . . .

There he lay, faceup in a pool of carbonated soda,
soaking into his red and black shirt, bubbling into his
    hair, spewing
into the fluorescent air, the boy who took her
away from Dean Koontz, drew her away from all that
    intrigue,
won her full attention.

Oh tell me, ye of little faith—
who is the master of mystery now?

Revelations

The crush rolled over her
like a truck
that's right, like her daddy's
red Ford pickup
all four tires
one after the other
till she felt completely
flattened

smushed by love.

The object of her affection?

Mr. Jasper
science teacher extraordinaire.

Maybe it was the way he pulled
his brown hair back in a ponytail
or the crazy ties he wore
or the way he hummed while
they dissected earthworms.

Maybe it was because
he told her she asked intelligent questions
something no one had ever said before.

Maybe, maybe . . .   maybe.
So here she was,
crushed as could be
tread marks all up and down her body
and she wondered . . .
would it be an intelligent question
to ask him how
to dissect the human heart?

In the Nurse's Office

In the nurse's office blood runs down his face
from the jagged cut above his swollen eye.
Tears and blood together, salty red embrace.

He couldn't see it coming, the knotted fist, the chase
that sent him spinning, spinning, face toward the sky.
In the nurse's office blood runs down his face.

He takes the blow, then stumbles, falls apace,
"fight, you stupid coward!" the ragged taunts rush by,
tears and blood together, salty red embrace.

He lurches into darkness, false as midnight's grace,
fluorescent lights blast in and out, comets gone awry.
In the nurse's office blood runs down his face.

She softly dabs his bruises, the wounds she can't erase,
sobs gather in his stomach, she'll never see him cry.
Tears and blood together, salty red embrace.

Skin and bone and sinew, one body in one place;
stars swim behind his eyelids, if only he could hide . . .
in the nurse's office blood runs down his face,
tears and blood together, salty red embrace.

What He Knew

God, she could kiss!
(It said so on the back of the stall
in the boys' room.)

And even though
his lips had never gotten
within an inch
or a mile
or even in the same neighborhood
as her lips . . .
he just knew.

How? He couldn't say.

But the knowing of it
wasn't easy on him
like the knowing
of his grandfather's
gentle pat on his back
or the knowing of
the way a stone
will skip across water.

So while she and all the others
walked past their lockers and laughed
and tossed their greetings about
the crowded hallway,
he slipped into the boys' room
and tenderly
washed her name
from the back of the stall,
caressed each letter
until it disappeared,
bit his bottom lip
until it bled.

Dreaming in Haiku

Because he loves math . . .
    haiku is a word problem
quantitative truths

Five . . . seven . . . then five
    images in syllables
x plus y is true

Words for whole numbers
    integers in small letters
greater than square roots

Because he loves math
    he loves haiku . . . equations
on soft white paper

He's dreaming haiku
    while he thinks about Sarah
haiku, same as math

It's just with Sarah
    nothing is mathematical . . .
only poetry

Homecoming

Normally, he hates being the shortest boy
in the tenth grade
shorter even than
most of the girls;

normally, short is a problem
to be such a shrimp
pee-wee
short stuff;

but tonight's not normal
tonight he's dancing with Laticia Sanders
the tallest girl
in the tenth grade;

normally, Laticia Sanders
walks down the hall
with her notebook in front
of her chest;

normally, his eyes
would only see her crossed arms

but tonight—like we said—
is not normal;

tonight, his eyes are exactly even
with Laticia's swaying breasts
that move in front of him
while she dances;

they've hypnotized him
enchanted him
cast a spell;

tonight is not normal
tonight, short is not a problem.

Elegies for Those We Lost Too Soon: Seven Acrostics

ONE—LIGHT MY FIRE

Jinxed, maybe that's the way he saw
it from his bathtub in Paris where his
melted heart stopped beating. At last,
Mojo Risin' to the highest high of all—
or maybe he just wanted to join his old friend
Rimbaud for a line of poetry, a quiet
retreat from his demons, who
insisted he was theirs, the Electric
Shaman. "Oh faithful spirit," cried the blood on the
open road, "the Lizard King has
no need to worry now."

TWO—THE KING

Ear toward the radio, my grandmother
listened as your sultry
velvet voice filled her kitchen, waxed perfect.
I listened too, easily. What was it she
said? Something about a
particular love, old, unfamiliar,
remote but still,
even to this day,
simmering beneath the surface,
limning the edges of her face
every time they play your song,
yesterday, tomorrow, then, now.

THREE—HAPPY BIRTHDAY, MR. PRESIDENT

Moonbeams hung soft
around her hair, a halo, a
ring of silver
illumination, a sulky
light. Should
you come to
notice the similiarities, the
moon, her face
on a black velvet
night, her satin
robe held loose
open above her knees
ebbing toward dawn.

FOUR—FEELIN' GOOD WAS EASY

Jacob fought an
angel, but
not you. You
invoked them,
sister. You made
Jacob and all the
others like him
put their souls in
loose bandannas and
irritated the hell out of those
nice boys—*tsk, tsk.*

FIVE—WAS IT TEEN SPIRIT?

Knows not what it means
underneath that hard-edged sheen
rivets from a classroom dream
tell me it's not what it seems.

Claim a princess, crown a queen
over, under, in between,
beside the ocean's bitter stream
a million floating stars agleam,
imagination skims the cream.
"Nevermind," the siren sings.

SIX—ELECTRIC LADYLAND

January always brings with
it a longing for you and
Monterey and all those
indivisible spangled stars.
Hey Joe! You startled the
endless wind and wailed right into
next year's blues.
Didn't you blaze a new
revolution? Didn't you sign
it with a planetary
X?

SEVEN—RUNNING ON FULL

Real life was a mirror for your
inviting smile; the screen a
victory of all those
everyday bits and pieces:
rainforests, rivers, reasons.
Poitier knew
how closely
one crosses the other, an
endless stream of precious
nuances. He called you
incandescent, and you were, like Saint
Xavier, savior of souls.

22 Homeroom

The Fat Girl

She's already reached into
her backpack four times
in fifteen minutes.

Four times, silently
at her metal desk against the wall,
she's slipped her hand
into the bright blue canvas pouch.

No one sees her, hears her
open the cellophane bags
Twinkies, M&M's, Chee-tos
her true companions.

Ever since they forgot her real name
somewhere around the fifth grade
she's certain
she's become invisible.

Without her real name
to identify her, then
who's to say she took
the missing peanuts
and creme-filled Oreos?

She thinks someday she'll shed
this skin she wears in layers
and float away
    down a river
    on a cloud

but right now it's all she can do
to stay away from that backpack.

Right now she's trying hard
to find her real name
sew it on her left pocket
in threads above her heart
so no one will forget again.

Cyberlove

he knew she was waiting
for him to get home
back to base
back to his computer
where she curled up
behind his screen
"cyberkitten"
that's all he knew to call her
it thrilled him
to watch the green letters
slip onto his screen
one by one as he
typed them in
careful not to hit the wrong key

he couldn't wait to get home
to find her message
he knew would be there
the one where she
would tell him
how her day had been
what she had for lunch
how much she missed him

he'd print it all out
on blue paper
tuck it into the special
notebook, blue too

on the front,
in plain black letters—
"cyberkitten"
cyberlove

Coach's Son

He's tall
almost six feet
broad shoulders
good for carrying
    the football
    the load
    the cheers
one hundred ninety pounds
he'll be a starter on the
varsity team next year
he'll need a tutor in math
he'd like to play the trombone
he loves to play Nintendo
he can play any position
all positions
but the hardest—
coach's son

his secret—
how much he loves
to hear his mama sing to him
. . . *rock-a-bye, my sleepy boy* . . .
as he drifts off to sleep.

Cheers

What if she *was* the captain
of the pep squad?
What about it?
What if she did enjoy leading the cheers,
flipping backward and forward
in front of the stadium,
yelling for the team?
Yelling for Phillip Mays, defensive end?

Push 'em back, push 'em back . . . waaaay back!

What if "the spirit" just took over
and picked her up,
tossed her over its shoulder
sang into her ears?

Can you dig it? Can you dig it?

What if the fight song
chanted in her mind day and night?

Go, team, go! Win, team, win!

Wasn't it all worth it?
Didn't it get her a date with Phillip Mays,
defensive end?
Wasn't that a victory?
Wasn't that one for the offense?

The Research Paper: A Sestina

My research paper this year is on polar bears,
inimitable denizens of the arctic circle,
who taught the Eskimos how to sleep in caves of ice.
It's said their fur is not really white, but clear
like glass, each strand a perfect crystal straw,
skin black to hold the heat of the fragile polar sun.

Perhaps in some other country there is too much sun,
like Mexico or Argentina, where right now a black bear's
traveling on the pampa, and tall grassy straw
bends beneath his heavy body in a circle
where he's slept; it's the same way in snow, a clear
field where polar bears leave circles in the ice.

I'll put a note in my bibliography about the ice,
how the bears sail out upon floes beneath the sun,
furred barges on the sea, as soon as winter clears—
they hunt for seals to feed their starving baby bears.
Or they wait beside a hole, a watery circle,
for the seal to emerge, then *whack,* the final straw.

Too bad the seal couldn't use a soda straw
to steal the needed breath instead of sticking her head
    above the ice!
Hey, why do the bears in Manitoba dance in a circle?
. . . I believe they are welcoming the fickle sun.
The encyclopedia doesn't say they're dancing, the
    bears . . .
but then again, the encyclopedia isn't always clear.

When I began all was clear, crystal clear
but there was a spit wad in the straw,
and I keep thinking how all this research bears
repeating, like the way Coca-Cola bubbles over ice,
and how everything, everything under the sun—
rocks, bubbles, poetry—comes back around to make a
    circle.

Each spring whoever my English teacher is draws a
    circle
on the blackboard and in the center, very clear,
puts "research," with rays extending, a chalky sun.
It's like all the times I drew the shortest straw,
sending goose bumps up my spine, cold as ice,
and now here I am alone, just me and the polar bears.

There's a clear voice in my head, "write about bears,"
while far to the north, a thin straw of light slips out of
    the freezing sun
and carves a rainbow in the ice of the bright white arctic
    circle.

A Circle of Light:
A Poem in Five Acts

PROLOGUE

Oh, let us call Saint Genesius
    his gentle touch
    his warm embrace
and neither judge nor jury be
    of these two fair
    of heart and face
of Tanner and Maria
    their story here unfolds
of love and loss and mystery
    Oh, let us not withhold
        our own forgivings.
Rather, keep them in this circle's light
and hold them, hold them, hold them tight.

ACT I

From the wings he watched. . . .
There she stood in the center of the stage,
    small in her white cotton gown
    eyes closed
    arms outspread
    facing the quiet seats
    dark in their emptiness
not a soul but he . . .

and she all alone
    beneath the bright Fresnels
    golden particles, charged,
    floated above her head in a spiral
    sifted into her body

through her gown
right into the very marrow of her bones.
He watched, unbelieving,
    as Juliet entered her
    a breath of air in search of a body
    slipped into her skin
    through the pores of her arms
    her face, her legs, her throat, her bare feet
so that when she opened her dark brown eyes
he saw she *was* Juliet
    through and through
        Shakespeare's daughter, Capulet.

He caught his breath and
the stage, the high school, the universe
became Verona and he,
Tanner Braden, became Romeo

to Maria Vasquez, his own Juliet,
there in the fiery circle of glittered light.

He fell, this new Montague,
to his knees, held the hem
of her cotton gown to his lips.

Oh, did the stars cross that night!
    An enchantment washed over them
    through all the acts, the rehearsals,
    the applause, a spell so strong
    it held them in its palm
    and kept them there all spring,
    dying in each other's arms a
    thousand times.

Such a confusion
    of nightingales and larks
    of day and night
    of dark and light.

ACT II

Maria had a secret that only Juliet knew
growing quietly
inside her, a tiny rose,
a bud.

A rose, a rose, would smell as sweet
by any other name. She watered
it with her tears.

Rose, she called it.
Rose, she called.
A rose she could not keep.
How could she keep it?
This secret, so small,
its fluttering petals soft inside her.

ACT III

Tanner had a bigger heart
than his ancestor Romeo . . .
    bigger than Verona
    bigger than the sun and sky and stars.
He thought a small heart could choose
to die, but not a large one,
and so it wasn't long, he left Romeo behind
on the printed page, the dusty stage,
and walked toward his Maria,

but even his big heart
was not enough to hold on to her.

Her parting wasn't sweet,
only sorrow.
So sudden was her going,
he lost his equilibrium

the hallways listed
words and numbers slid
off the classroom chalkboards
into their trays, beside the erasers
his teachers' words floated in the chalky air
incomprehensible, silent.

A large heart yearns larger
    like the tide for the moon its mate
    calls to her, moans in its longing,
    reaches out in whispered dreams
    and sleepless nights
    howls into its pillow, sodden.

Such wanting only a large heart knows.

ACT IV

This rose, closed.
This secret, gone.
This sorrow, new
    and old
    and ancient
    as roses.

ACT V

Maybe tomorrow she will tell him,
if she can.

Maybe tomorrow she will
take his hand and pull him
into that circle of light, grown older,
upon the deserted stage,
her white gown
stained red from
her Romeo's own rapier.

Maybe tomorrow she
will know forgiveness,
and maybe he will take her in his arms
and defy the empty soulless seats,
their remonstrances.

Maybe he will cup her face
in his hands and weep.

Maybe the glittering light
will hold in its warm and soft embrace
its forgotten Romeo and Juliet,
one Montague, one Capulet.

EPILOGUE

For now we hope for maybe,
    its soothing balm
    its smooth caress.
For now we hope for grief,
    its swelling tears
    its tenderness.

Oh, how we hope for Tanner and Maria,
    their shattered, broken hearts.
Oh, let us hope for nightingales,
    Oh, let us pray for larks.

Ms. Dove and Mr. Edgars

Couldn't let anyone know
they loved each other so
each morning he stood
by his window in Room 225
saw her pull up in the parking lot
step out of her blue Toyota Camry
arms full of papers
his heart ran out to meet her
while he stood behind the pane
she always glanced his way
then hurried to her class

during break in the teachers' lounge
she dropped a quarter and a dime
into the soda machine
he stood behind her
rattling the change in his pocket
not a single word betrayed them
after she left
he tried to find something
to quench his thirst

all year they played
this quiet charade
so that no one
would ever suspect

and every day he wondered
would it be so bad
if he took her hand
in front of everyone
whispered in her ear
rested his palm
on the small of her back?

The Yearbook Photographer

He's like smoke
that narrow boy

    here
there   gone
    where

he wafts among the smiles
    slips between the covers
        slides along the edge

    click!

    flash!

he's hard to find . . .

        like smoke

he burns your eyes . . .

        like smoke

he sees
    say "cheese"

    Caught!
    (you,
        not him)

in black and white

        and gray . . .

    like smoke.

Dumpling

When her daddy
ran his rough hands down her blouse
all smelling of old motor oil and gasoline
and said, "I sure got me a dumpling,"
shoot, from then on
she couldn't get dumplings
out of her head.

She saw them everywhere, their aroma rising up—

In World Geography, it was the Greek Isles on the map
her teacher pulled down in front of the chalkboard
floating there in the Mediterranean Sea
their biscuit shapes atop the salty water.

In Science, it was the bar of pink soap
at the bottom of the coppery sink
slick from a thousand sets of hands hands
and more hands.

Until finally, even hands, the fat hands of her
band director clutching his thin baton,
the chubby hands of Terence Paton
drumming on his desk in Spanish II,
the hands she folded into a prayer she
couldn't speak, her father's hands,
all, all looked like dumplings.
Not even the green and white Oxydol that
she stole from her mother's washroom
and took with her to the shower
could wash it all away.
No matter how much

she scrubbed,
didn't matter atall,
she never could get
that old gasoline smell to go away.

Notes Passed Back and Forth in U.S. History Class, Seventh Period

Hey there, brown-eyed girl
    the empty desk next to mine
has your name on it.

You! Boy with the desk
    did you have cornflakes for lunch?
Where did your bus stop?

Hmm, hmm, girlie-o
    I'm keeping this desk open
bring your attitude.

Desk Boy! Take a hike
    take your luscious brown freckles
take your cutie-pie eyes . . .

Take a hint—"hint, hint."
    The empty desk keeps calling
this heart keeps falling.

No way no way no . . .
    If I moved into that desk
my brain might shut down.

You've got it all wrong
    it would help you concentrate
this is SuperDesk.

SuperDesk would keep
    me shielded from your wispy
breath upon my neck?

Come see for yourself—
   no strings attached, brown-eyed girl.
Free! One empty desk!

Oh, freckle-faced boy . . .
   you take this kiss instead—wrapped
in silver paper.

The Driver's License

Ever since she got her driver's license,
since that day, palms sweating,
almost slipping off the steering wheel—
    Officer Graham, crisp as a cracker, in his brown
    Department of Public Safety uniform
    with the silver badge on his left chest,
    five points on the star, like Wyatt Earp,
    sitting beside her in the vinyl seat, making notes
    on a clipboard, same brown as his uniform,
    sweat on his upper lip—
since that day she parallel-parked on Third Street
    right in front of the Ben Franklin that had been
        closed for
    a hundred years, or at least a dozen years, its
        closing
    almost killing her grandaddy, who worked there
    all his adult life, selling ribbons and buttons
    to women with black and gold Singers in the
    corners of their living rooms—
since that day when she remembered to use her
    blinkers
as she approached her turns, both left and right,
remembered to place her hands at ten and two o'clock,
remembered to slow down on the yellow,
speed up a little when she changed lanes,
approach with caution at the railroad tracks,
    Whew!!!
Ever since then, she's remembered to wear
her nicest underwear.

"What if you have a wreck and have to be taken to the
    hospital?"
her mother said, over and over. . . .

Shoot, if she could do all of the above, could pass that
    driving test
with a only a couple of points taken off, "just because no
    one's perfect,"
according to Officer Graham,
then, by George, she'd wear perfect underwear.

'Cause the way her mother made it sound,
if she didn't have on clean underwear and had a wreck?
The ambulance driver might take a look and say,
"Sorry, her underwear's too dirty. Let's leave her here in
    the ditch."

My Lord, it was just not worth the embarrassment.
And besides, it was such a small thing,
and if it got her mother off her back, all the better.
Clean underwear was an easy price to pay
for getting her where she needed to go.

Apply Yourself!

"Apply yourself!" was all he ever heard,
as if he could wrap himself around his homework
    like a Band-Aid around a cut
as if he could glue his fingers to his Spanish
        vocabulary words,
    paper feathers on his fingertips
as if he could nail his palms to Economics
as if he could plug his whole being into the good grade
    machinery
as if he could tape his head to the linoleum
as if he could paste his butt to the desk
as if he could spread his gray matter onto the test sheet
    like peanut butter on toast
as if algorithms and battles and presidents and
    theorems and scales and pep rallies and
    maps and cosines and Bunsen burners and
    hurricane charts and bills of rights and
    dangling participles and dress codes and
    all that filled his notebook could stick to his thin body
        like flies to flypaper, his fragile wings
        pinned to the poisonous strip
    as if all that matters and will matter
    is to add it all up and fill out the application . . .
as if that mattered at all, as if that mattered
    at all . . . or all at once . . .
as if that was all that mattered.

What He Took with Him

His Pink Floyd T-shirt and two more,
a week's worth of clean boxer shorts,
his toothbrush and half a tube of Colgate
with baking soda, a stick of Old Spice
Original, same brand his father used,
forty-one dollars and some change,
a fresh pack of Camel Lights in a box,
a book of matches, some mismatched socks,
the Tao Te Ching, one blue marble, his mother's heart,
his father's broken one, all their dreams.

What he left behind:
the cream-colored cat, wild in her loneliness;
his CD collection, quiet; the air,
wondrous for his being there.

The Science Fair

She knew where all their nests were . . .

mourning doves—the grove of pines outside the band
    hall
Carolina wrens—tucked inside the S and Os of the
    school's name,
boat-tailed grackles—in the cottonwood tree beside
    the garbage Dumpster
MacGillivray's warblers—the pair of live oaks by the
    bus stop
pigeons—the gutters along the pitched roof
black-capped chickadees—in the boxed brick grooves
    of the gymnasium
mockingbirds—the tallest branches of the tallest
    pines
indigo buntings—invisible
starlings—grassy field beside the track
swallows—among the broad beams of the back
    entrance
brown thrashers—deep in the fallen pine needles
    outside the science labs
jays—atop the electrical transformer behind the
    cafeteria
red-winged blackbirds—just above the concrete
    pilings of the portico

in her pockets—
    sunflower seeds

in her eye—
    wings.

The Twirling Queen of Dogwood, Texas

It was as if there was a whispering inside her,
or maybe it was from a pine tree.
It could have come to her in her sleep one night
when she was three or four, curled up tight, one
arm around her stuffed rabbit, Bitsy, the other
beneath her pillow and she, smelling
of pink bubbles from her bath,
floated atop the sheets, ear to the ceiling—
maybe it was then.

Anyway, it spoke up loud and clear:

    Go forth and twirl!

And by God, that's what she did.

At first she twirled her fork and knife,
then odd twigs from the backyard trees,
any object that was straight and narrow
and lightweight—a forgotten curtain rod in the
back of her mother's closet, the towel bar that
fell down one night when her big brother, Bruce,
tried to do chin-ups after brushing his teeth,
pens and pencils, crayons, even Malibu
Barbie with her tiny high heels and bright fuchsia
    surfboard.

Without even knowing she was doing them,
she perfected figure eights and knuckle spins.
And Bitsy stared in appreciation.
She was the twirling queen of her household,
the happy genius.

Then on her sixth birthday, her Aunt Joleen,
bless her heart, the heartbreaker of Kilgore,
who had won more beauty pageants in East
Texas than the Colonel had fried drumsticks,
and been married as often,
gave her the most perfect pink baton,
and even showed her a few basic tricks,
which Aunt Joleen exclaimed came
as naturally as bees came
to honey.

Some things just go together—you know,
clouds with rain, potatoes with gravy,
ostriches with sand. That's how she was
with that pink baton.
A perfect fit.

And it wasn't long before Aunt Joleen had
her signed up for lessons and pageants
and parades and competitions.
My gosh, pretty soon she was the
twirling queen of the piney woods,
destined for greatness.

Which opened its doors when she entered
Dogwood High School. Even though the
football team wasn't worth squat, people
began to show up at the Friday night games just to
watch the halftime show.

She never let them down, no she didn't.
As soon as the team hobbled off the
field and the band lined up beneath the
goalposts, out she strutted, skin-tight sequins
hugging her tight body in the school colors,
red and gold. Sister, she was a sight
to behold.

Everyone in the stadium held their breath,
even the visitors, when she took to the field
with her golden batons—the original pink one
was tucked safely in her bedroom closet with Bitsy—
not one, not two, not three, but four
batons, made especially for her by a
company up in Chicago, gold-plated and
engraved with her name in script,
two in each hand, spinning so fast
they looked like propellers, as if any minute
she might lift right off the turf and helicopter
into the black sky with the circling nighthawks.

Whoooeeee!!!

So was it any wonder, when that movie company
from Hollywood chose Dogwood as the setting
for a major motion picture, starring major motion
picture stars, that she, the twirling queen,
would be featured in the opening and closing credits?
Not one person in Dogwood was surprised at all,
in fact all of a sudden it seemed like she was related
to half the county (and if you counted Aunt Joleen's
many husbands, then she sort of was, in a way,
    remotely
related to lots of them). You could hear them
talking at the drugstore—"You know, she's my cousin by
marriage," or "Her aunt was my sister-in-law for a
    spell," or
"My daughter used to be in her first twirling class,
which was taught by my mother's best friend."

It was just flat amazing how genealogical that girl
    could be.
And everyone was so, so proud to be related to her,
or to be her neighbor. The mayor even proposed a

petition to change the slogan of the town, "Dogwood,
    Heart of the Piney Woods,"
to "Dogwood, Home of the Twirling Queen."
That's how impressed everyone was, especially
    Aunt Joleen,
who was about to pop out of her support hose with
    pride.

But here's the thing: once that movie came out, with
    the major
motion picture stars and the opening and closing
    credits, with
the twirling queen strutting across the screen in her red
    and gold
sequins, she heard that old voice, the one she heard way
    back
when she was three or so and still slept with Bitsy, that
    calling.
And this time it said the same thing, only different—

Go forth and twirl!

Before the closing credits ended, before her
last fantastic leap on film, golden batons
whirling across the screen, before the lights came
back up and someone might see her, she took a deep
    breath
and walked out of the Palace Theater,
all decked out in her drop-dead-gorgeous
premiere gown especially designed by Nina,
who normally designed wedding gowns for local
    brides,
but was so happy to sew anything that wasn't white,
peach, or aqua with ruffles and
puffy sleeves that she was tickled when Aunt Joleen
commissioned this one for the opening,

and didn't even charge extra for the silk lining.
There she went, through the double doors,
shimmering from head to toe, one spaghetti
strap sliding off her shoulder, she slid
into the night air, cool and crisp, perfect,
looking fit for the Oscars.

She stopped only long enough to pick up her batons
from the backseat of her daddy's El Dorado,
and walked to the high school football stadium.
It was dark there, but she could imagine the burning
      lights,
the smell of popcorn and sweat, the blare of the
      trumpets.
She stood in the middle of the field, two batons in each
hand, and began to spin. First one, then the other, until
all four were spinning—faster, faster, faster.

Her heart raced, she wasn't sure she could do it,
she didn't know if she could let go . . . she closed her
      eyes,
then, one, two, three, four, she released
the spinning batons into the sky—

She stopped and looked up as they flew past
the risers, past the lights, past the moon and stars,
and disappeared from sight. . . .

   Here you are!

she yelled. Then, without looking back,
she quietly walked out of the stadium, across the empty
parking lot, and stopped. She smiled. She thought she
heard someone say *thank you* but it could have been
her own small voice, yes it could, it had that tiny edge of
a drawl. But who can tell for sure?

It's been said that the next night, she and Aunt Joleen
    watched
the major motion picture three times, once for luck,
twice for a good laugh, and the third time for
the charm of it all. As for those four batons,
with their graven script and the special gold plating?
There are lots of theories: one is that a flock of
passing geese grabbed them as they spun
into the sky and carried them off to Canada
for the summer. Some say that they landed
in the Trinity River just a few miles from
town. Others assume that
they're simply lodged in the thick floor of the
pine forest, hidden beneath generations of
pine needles. Treasure hunters sometimes
dig around out there on Sunday afternoons,
their metal detectors tuned to low frequencies
humming beneath the trees.

One thing's certain—they're gone. And so is
the twirling queen for that matter. One day
she simply slipped out of town without a
word to anyone, not even her many
relatives. Only thing she took with her
was Bitsy and a big ol' hug from Aunt Joleen,
who stood beside the Greyhound bus
and waved good-bye long after the bus
pulled away.

Where she went Aunt Joleen's not
saying, only that she had a calling and
followed it. She might be in Boston
studying medicine. Could be she went
to Hollywood to meet up with those
major motion picture folks. Perhaps
she's off in Florida working with

underprivileged children? It's a mystery
for sure. Now and then someone
declares a sighting, usually in the same sentence
as Elvis, even though he was no twirler, which
gave one of the local artists the idea to
paint her portrait on black velvet replete with
real red and gold sequins and hang it in the
lobby of Dogwood City Hall right next to
the portrait of Stephen F. Austin, another
visionary from those parts.

She'll probably go back there someday.
Maybe. Most likely. And there's a real
good chance that no one will recognize
her, which will be fine by her. Because the
reason she left, the reason she stayed
away so long: It's hard to be
a twirling queen and a person too.
    Amen, said the voice,
        Amen.

Night Mares

Remember the mares of night,
the way they gallop in circles
on the looped rug beside the bed.
My favorite, the palomino, aglow
in the crack of light from beneath the door. She
calls to her foal, a piebald,
her eyes black as coal.
See how they pause at the brink—moonbeam puddles,
pools on the bathroom tiles,
each dip of their heads a thirsty prayer.
Remember the paints and bays, the zebra duns,
their hooves clattering across the wood
floor of the dining room. My grandmother
unfastens her pearls, coils them on the glass
of her cherry dressing table,
gently unbraids her hair—
a brush, a comb, a knot of silver hair.
What is there to give for
dreams of chestnuts and
Appaloosas, dapples and grays,
an open palm of sweet green grass?
The mares of night—
remember them?

PART TWO

Study Hall:
Writing What We Long For

Homeroom

As I mentioned earlier, this is the one poem in the book that is not about a particular person. Instead, it's my tribute to poetry in general and the home that it has always provided me. By that I mean that, regardless of what is going on around me in the big outside world, I can find solace in both reading and writing poetry. It gives me a space that's all my own, and I can make of it whatever I wish. Of course, I can bring other poets and their work into the space, just as I can bring friends into my actual home. It's not all that different. And just as unwelcome guests and circumstances sometimes appear in my life, they also appear in my poetry. They show up as emotions usually—anger, frustration, sadness—all those less-than-positive guests who knock on our doors at different times in our lives. The challenge then becomes how to deal with them. I've learned that if I turn my back on them, they usually knock harder next time. Better to go ahead and invite them in and address their complaints.

When I was in school, we had a daily homeroom. Today I think these classes are called advisory periods, or something like that. I'm sorry the old-fashioned name is disappearing. In homeroom we were never divided by ability or talent, only by alphabet. We didn't have to do anything special. All we had to do was show up, and there was quite a bit of comfort in that. It was always just a short class in which we heard the daily announcements and sort of geared up for the oncoming day. I always thought of homeroom the way a homing pigeon might think of its nest—the one place where nothing was expected of me. I like to think of poetry in this way too— that it doesn't matter if the poem works or not, that it's not going to be graded or evaluated, that whatever I put on the page is great. And if I paint it some weird color, well, who cares?

The longing?
To write.

1. Buy yourself a notebook or journal in which to put your poems. You may be like me and write many of your pieces on the computer. If so, print them out and paste them into the notebook. Make the notebook wonderful. Decorate it. Give it a title. Love it.

2. Read as much poetry as you can. Don't worry about whether or not you "get it." Let it soak in. Read it out loud, as it's intended.

3. Hold your own poetry readings with your friends. Have great refreshments. Applaud after every poem.

4. Write a poem a day. Take a look at David Lehman's *The Daily Mirror: A Journal in Poetry,* which is a collection of poems he wrote over the course of three years as a challenge to himself to write a daily poem no matter what his circumstances. He wrote on trains, in restaurants, before bed, wherever he found himself with a piece of paper and a pencil. You can do this too.

5. Write all the time.

Lost in the Blues

Go to a dance or a concert, and you will almost always spot someone who is playing air guitar along with the band. I'm married to a guitar player, and I know for a fact that guitar players often "play" even when they don't have their actual guitars in their hands. And lots of non-guitar players do a similar thing. The boy I had a crush on in high school played the cornet, and he would sometimes play the "air cornet," almost as if he were taking a break on some jazz tune that only he could hear. His idol was Dizzy Gillespie, the famous jazz trumpeter. As a very small child, I used to have an imaginary horse. For a while he was my best friend. He even rode in the car with me. Air instruments and air animals are more common than we think, and they provide lots of material for poems and stories.

The longing?
To imagine.

1. If you could imagine being someone else, who would it be? If you could imagine being very good at something, what would it be? What is it you dream of doing? Write a poem about that. Then write a poem

about what it might take to get you there. Write it in steps.

2. If you could meet someone special, who would it be? Write about your encounter with that person. What if my character, Jimmy Haliburton, actually got to meet Jimi Hendrix? What would he ask him? What if they could have a jam session? Would they trade licks? Would they wail into the night?

3. It's imagination that helps us find out what we're supposed to do with our lives. It helps us to see possibilities. And just as important, it often helps us to solve problems. I really wish we could have "daydreaming classes" or "creativity classes" right along with Geometry and English. Wouldn't that be fun? Wouldn't it be useful? If you could design your own school, what classes would you include? Which ones would you leave out?

4. In this poem, there are two names: the name of my character and the name of a famous rock star. Jimmy Haliburton and Jimi Hendrix. I intentionally made them sound alike to give them a superficial bond. Naming is a powerful act. It has to be done carefully. When we use the name of a famous person, we get an instant image of that person in our heads. Likewise, when we create a character, the name can give us at least a fuzzy image of who that person is. It usually, but not always, tells us a person's gender. It sometimes delegates the person to a time period. My mother-in-law's name is Wilma, and her sister's was Eunice. Those were popular names in the 1920s when they were born, but you rarely hear them now. A name can give us an idea of the person's ethnicity—race, culture, background. My friend Mohammed runs a Turkish restaurant. His name told me that he was

probably Muslim. Write a poem in which you name the character. When you're finished, go back and change the name and see if it affects the way the poem turns out. Put a famous person in the poem. Be careful with names.

The Tattoo Dragon

One Sunday morning while I was sitting in church, a young woman walked in and sat in the pew beside me. She had the most magnificent dragon tattoo on her leg. It looked exactly the way I described it in the poem. It even seemed to shimmer when she moved her leg. I couldn't take my eyes off that dragon, and to this day I could not tell you what the sermon was about. But I very definitely remember the woman and her wondrous tattoo. Seeing it brought up all kinds of questions: Did she have it done in one sitting? Didn't it hurt? What made her choose a dragon? Why in the world would she do it?

The longing?
To individuate or set ourselves apart.

1. Public places such as churches, concerts, skating rinks, arcades, bowling alleys, athletic arenas, and schoolyards are great places to observe people. When you watch people, take note of their clothing, their jewelry, a birthmark, a tattoo, or something else that sets them apart. Use that odd thing as a centerpiece for a poem.

2. Write about someone who loves being a member of a particular group—the drummer in the band, the cheerleader, a member of the choir, or the French club—then list the ways in which he or she loves it.

3. Sometimes we peg people and force them into a group: the slow readers, the nerds, the preps. Once someone is classified, it's hard to become unclassified. Write about someone who hates being a member of group—then list the ways in which he or she hates it.

4. It seems like a dragon tattoo would make you feel fairly powerful—like a dragonslayer. How would something like a pierced eyebrow make you feel? What about a new dress? How about a black trenchcoat?

5. My character, Patty Lopez, chose to have the tattoo engraved on her leg. Some of us, however, have distinguishing characteristics that we didn't choose—a cleft lip or a horrible scar, maybe our clothing is ragged and our shoes full of holes. Maybe we don't have access to a shower and the distinguishing "mark" is our body odor. And so our individuation is not an asset but a liability. In that case, the longing to be the same might outweigh the longing to be unique. Write about someone like that.

Good Job, Buddy

One night my youngest son, Cooper, who was fourteen at the time, and I went to the grocery store. It was very late and all the workers in the store were stocking the shelves and the rock-and-roll music was up very loud. As Cooper and I went down one of the aisles, he suddenly stood on the back of the grocery cart and popped a wheelie. It was such a feat of strength and agility that it made an impression on me.

As we went along, I also realized that these late hours were really the domain of the young—folks who were finishing up late shifts at work, the young stockers, people who were heading home after a party. I felt out of place in my middle-agedness. However, I was dazzled by the young folks all around me. I also remembered how, as a waitress in my late teens, I used to stop by the grocery store after work and dig through the paperback books in search of something wonderful to read. Cooper with his daring wheelie, the boys stocking the shelves, the young waitress—all provided seeds for this narrative poem.

The longing?
For attention.

1. Do you remember a time when you tried to get someone's attention and couldn't? What did you do? How did you feel? What finally happened? Write about it.

2. Some of us go to great and often dangerous lengths to get the attention of another person. Do you know someone like that? A daredevil? Write about that person.

3. Sometimes a person commits a crime as a cry for attention. Do some research. Read the newspaper. Can you find someone like that? Write about it. You can even take the news article and transform it into a poem. Use some of the lines from the article as starters. Be sure to load the poem with details.

4. Some people make an art out of getting attention. All of us have met someone who dominates every situation. Try to figure out what is behind that person's need to be the center of attention. Start the poem with "He was always the center of the circle . . ." and keep going.

5. On the other hand, think of a time when the last thing you needed was attention. Maybe you didn't read your assignment for English, and the teacher called on you to talk about the plot of the story. Write about those times too.

6. I live with two Manx cats and a fish who have several ingenious ways of getting my attention. Think about pets and write about the ways they get you to meet their needs. Who is in charge?

Revelations

For many of us, the first person we fall in love with is a teacher, especially if that teacher seems to take a particularly warm interest in us, or helps us discover something important about ourselves. That's just what happened to my hero in this poem. Has it ever happened to you?

The longing?
For recognition.

1. Have you ever had a time when a teacher applauded you for something you did well? When you write about it, be specific. What were you wearing? How old were you? Did you feel embarrassed? How did your classmates react? Did you feel like you were floating? Did it change the course of your life?

2. Has there ever been a really special adult in your life—a teacher, an instructor, a neighbor? Write about that person and your special connection to each other.

3. Have you ever confused someone's recognition for something else? Maybe a romantic interest? Maybe you thought someone liked you when all he or she really

wanted was to be friends? Write about the confusion. How did it start? What happened when you discovered the mixed signals. Write about the mixed signals themselves.

4. Giving a compliment is sometimes hard, but often accepting one is even harder. A compliment can have the effect of putting us on the spot. Write a poem about receiving an unexpected compliment and how you or your character reacted.

5. Have you ever received a trophy or an award? Do you know someone else who has? My grandmother Marge had what seemed like a zillion bowling trophies. They took up an entire shelf in her dining room and, boy, did they ever tell me some things about my grandmother—that she loved being on a team, that she was competitive, that she was tough and feisty. They also reminded me what a terrible bowler I was, so they were mixed symbols for me. Do you know someone who has lots of awards and trophies? What do they say to you about that person, as well as about yourself?

In the Nurse's Office

One of my best friends is a school nurse. I keep urging her to write her memoirs because so many things happen in her office that the rest of us never hear about. She's the keeper of a million secrets.

The longing?
To forget.

1. Have you ever experienced or witnessed a fight at school? Try to recapture all the details. Write it first as a newspaper article. Then write it as if you were testifying in a trial as an eyewitness. You might even approach it from the perpetrator's point of view. Try to see it from as many angles as possible, including the school nurse, principal, fireman, doctor, victim, or whoever might have been present.

2. Television has become a powerful presence in our daily lives. Hardly anyone in the world could have escaped seeing the World Trade Towers come crashing down on September 11, 2001. Poetry is often a response to tragedy, and right after the event, thou-

sands of people sent poems to their newspapers and posted them on Web sites as attempts to express their grief and fear. Poet Laureate Billy Collins did an interview on National Public Radio on the afternoon of the eleventh, and he called the absence of the towers "monuments of air." It was his way of honoring the forever-changed landscape. When we are harmed, whether it's on a global level or on the street level, we are changed in large ways. Were you changed by an event you witnessed on television? Did you feel removed? Do you remember where you were and what you were doing when it happened? Write about that. If you could build a monument, what would you call it?

3. This poem is a villanelle, a very structured kind of form. It has nineteen lines altogether, broken into five three-line stanzas and a final four-line stanza. The first and third lines in each stanza end in a rhyme. Lines 1, 6, 12, and 18 are the same. And lines 3, 9, 15, and 19 are the same. This repetition is what gives the villanelle its force. It's almost as if the reiterations help us get the poet's message. The most famous villanelle is probably Dylan Thomas's beautiful and powerful "Do Not Go Gentle into That Good Night."

   While most of my poetry is done in free verse—that is, it's free of forms such as rhymes and meter and specific numbers of stanzas—sometimes the chaotic nature of the subject matter calls for an orderly form to help the poet and the reader make sense of the event. Having the safe structure of the form allows us to howl at the moon. It gives us the boundaries we need to push against. Use this form to write something you feel strongly about. Try writing a "protest poem." Allen Ginsberg was the master of protest poetry, but he wrote in free verse. Do you think his message might have been clearer if he had used the villanelle?

4. The villanelle also provides a challenge where rhyme is concerned. Some authorities will claim that "formula poetry" is only for those who can't control free verse. On the other hand, those who write in the forms claim that the masterful poet can use the form to create a more powerful message. I personally like the challenge of both. The problem with most rhyme, however, is that many of us have only experienced it in nursery rhymes or children's books, and so it's difficult to write about a serious subject without diminishing it in a sing-songy way, like Mother Goose. The villanelle is one kind of rhyming poem that does not have that feel. Take a tragic or scary event and try writing it as a villanelle.

5. Not all moments that we want to forget are scary. Some are embarrassing. Write a villanelle about an embarrassing occasion—one you wish would go away forever.

What He Knew

I once had a deep, deep crush on my best friend's boyfriend. No one ever knew about it but me. I'm glad I kept it to myself. I don't remember the boy, but I still have the friend.

The longing?
For responsibility.

1. Have you ever had to cover for a friend? Write a poem about that. Be very specific about the details. Describe the situation, what you had to do, whether or not the truth ever came out, how it affected you.

2. Do you know someone who has a terrible reputation? If you could help offset it one little bit, what would you do?

3. Write about something you know about, even though you've never experienced it.

4. Find a funny line on a bathroom wall and use that as the first line for a poem.

5. Have you ever had to prove yourself in order to gain something? Write about that.

Dreaming in Haiku

I used to love my English classes. Loved the stories we read, loved analyzing them, loved the way the object followed the verb. But I was never too hot in math. One day I was watching a friend make some quick calculations on paper, and I realized that he loved doing them. He absolutely adored math. Then I began to wonder what it must be like for someone who loved math to have to sit through English. That's when it occurred to me that a lot of poetry is very mathematical—it has a certain number of syllables or a particular rhyme scheme or the accent has to fall on just the right beat. Thinking about that was the impetus behind this poem.

The longing?
To solve a problem or figure something out.

1. I love to dig through textbooks—geography, history, biology, chemistry, math, it doesn't matter what the subject matter—and find all those fat, juicy words. Take a look at my poem. Who would've thought you could include all that math vocabulary in a poem? Write haikus for world history and see what you get.

2. Writing is definitely one way to make discoveries, solve a problem, or come to a realization. A journal is often the domain for this kind of writing. However, beyond the journal, poetry is an excellent realm for "showing" the answer to a puzzle. Write a poem using the subject matter for each of your classes, regardless of what they are, and see if you don't make a discovery. For example, if you are taking American History, write a poem about one of the people you are studying. Let's take George Washington: Could you write about George and his false teeth? Doesn't he feel more human, and less heroic, when we think of his teeth? Or you could be more serious and write about the worries he had over his freezing soldiers at Valley Forge. What things surrounding that awful event might have bothered him? The distance from their families, the rampant disease, the scarcity of food and clothing, the perils that faced them? If you're taking Chemistry, pretend you are a master chemist and use one of the lab experiments from your textbook to make a big discovery. It might sound silly, but try it anyway.

3. Like the villanelle, the haiku has a form. The most traditional haiku has three lines; the first has five syllables, the second has seven, and the third has five again. The best haiku paints a picture, like a small snapshot, of whatever it is you're writing about. When you are trying out haiku, be sure you concentrate on the image of your subject.

4. We've all had the experience of being somewhere we didn't want to be, like the math lover in the English class or the bull in the china shop. Think about being in a place where you aren't entirely comfortable, but then make the best of the situation—make a

discovery anyway. Cop the attitude that "all things happen for a reason," then figure out why you were there in the first place. What were you supposed to get out of it?

Homecoming

My oldest son has a close friend who is very short, much shorter than the other boys in his class. Now I'm a short person, but it seems like being short has a whole different meaning for boys, just as being tall has a different meaning for girls. The thing is, sometimes the universe gives us a bum rap. So, one day while I was thinking about my son's friend, it occurred to me, "Geez, there's nothing that he can do about being short . . . so what would be a fair and just thing for him, something that could only happen *because* he was short?" The answer was this poem.

The longing?
For justice.

1. Have you ever been in a situation in which you were cheated out of something that you deserved or felt you deserved? What was that like? How did you feel? Write about it.

2. Do you, or does someone you know, have a physical liability or a distinguishing mark that separates you

from the "norm"? What is it? How does it affect you? Has anything wonderful ever happened because of it?

3. Write about someone who doesn't go by the rules.

4. Was there ever a time when you stood up for someone who was being treated unfairly? What did you do? What do you wish you had done? If you could go back in time, what would you change?

5. History is full of injustices: slavery, hunger, poverty. Today, special news shows on television do whole programs on people who have been treated unfairly, or who seem to have been. Pay attention to the news, both on television and in magazines and papers. Find a story that deals with a seeming injustice and write a poem.

6. Sometimes life brings unexpected joys and sorrows. Surely by the time you are a teenager, you've experienced both. Write poems about sudden events that either brought you happiness or grief.

7. All of the major religions have the equivalent of the Golden Rule: *Do unto others as you would have them do unto you.* Buddhists believe in *karma,* the idea that in order to receive good in your life, you must be good. Have you experienced karma, where the good guy wins and the bad guy gets what he has coming? Take a look. Write about it.

8. For some reason, we give our celebrities breaks that we don't give to each other. For example, we're often able to turn the other cheek when the star athlete gets busted for drug use or the movie star gets off easy for abusing her children. How do you explain that? Is it fair?

Elegies For Those We Lost Too Soon: Seven Acrostics

One evening my husband and I were watching a documentary on The Doors, the rock-and-roll band from the early 1960s, and their charismatic young lead singer, Jim Morrison. When I was a teenager, I danced to his deep, soulful voice and learned to drive while his lyrics boomed through the car's radio. But I never knew much about him except that he had died in a bathtub in Paris of a heart attack. Some assumed it was a drug overdose. No one really knows for sure. After watching the show, I began to think about all the other young artists and athletes who died long before they should have. It made me want to take a look at their lives.

The longing?
To honor.

1. Make a list of famous people you admire or are intrigued by. Do some research about them. If they are no longer alive, write a short elegy. An elegy honors someone who has passed. The word is closely related to *eulogy,* a tribute commonly given at a funeral.

If they are still alive, write an ode. I've found that if I'm experiencing a bit of a writer's block, I can do some research and it helps me move past the block because the research itself gives me something to say and to write about.

2. Not too many years ago, a friend of mine lost her son in an automobile accident. Not knowing what to say or how to react in her presence, I wrote a poem about her son and my experience of him. It was my gift to her, a respectful remembrance of a young man who should not have died so early. Anne Lamott, in her book *Bird by Bird,* says that all writing should be a gift to someone. Nowhere is this more true than in elegies.

3. These poems are simple acrostics—the first letter of each line, read vertically, spells out the name of the person who is being elegized. There are all kinds of acrostics, many of which are very complicated. They are a great way to play with language, and they have the effect of dissolving a writer's block. Study Edgar Allan Poe's acrostics for examples of some great acrostic poetry.

4. Make a list of the people who mean quite a bit to you. Write an ode honoring at least one of them. An ode is a poem that exalts, elevates, or praises someone or something. Concentrate on the small things that make that person special. Then give the poem to him or her. I give poems as birthday gifts, Christmas gifts, valentines. They sure beat ties and candy, and they don't cost as much, either. Pablo Neruda was the best at writing odes for common things. He wrote odes to pepper and salt, a watermelon, a cat. Find something small and everyday and write an ode. Write a collection.

5. It would have been easy for me, in these poems, to dwell on each person's death, especially since it could be argued that all these people died by their own hand. However, I tried to see, through my memory of them as well as through research, what they were like in life. It's easy to be fascinated by death; but it's more interesting to be fascinated by life. Write an elegy that does not mention or dwell on death, but rather on what the person represented in life.

The Fat Girl

Many people are affected by eating disorders, including anorexia and bulimia. Beginning with our hunter-gatherer ancestors, our relationship with food has been complex; not only is food necessary, but the way we treat it is filled with rituals and superstitions. We all know someone who is either painfully thin or incredibly overweight.

The images from the media don't help. We're constantly bombarded with ads that assure us that happiness (or at least a party) can be found in a particular kind of burger or a certain brand of soft drink. In those same ads, the people indulging in this junk food are all icons of health—slim, tan, and with perfect white teeth. Is there a problem with this picture? Most of us don't fit into the images displayed by movie stars and models and so it is very hard to be happy with the way we are.

The longing?
For respect.

1. All of us have moments when we feel completely invisible to the outside world, when it seems as if no one knows who we are. Perhaps you've had a teacher who can't remember your name. Or maybe you have a sib-

ling who demands so much attention your parents hardly notice you. Maybe you're uncomfortable being noticed. What if nobody knew your name? What would that be like?

2. The names John Doe and Jane Doe are frequently given to unidentified victims of crime, homelessness, poverty, or mental illness. Create your own John or Jane Doe and write a narrative poem about him or her.

3. Lots of rituals surround meals, especially during holidays. What is your favorite meal? Who prepares it? Do you help in the preparation? Write about a typical or an atypical meal at your house and the people involved. Be specific. Use all of your five senses. Include the dog beside the table.

4. Look at a bunch of food ads, then look at a bunch of fashion ads. Write a poem using slogans from the ads.

Cyberlove

The Internet has opened up a whole new way for us to find each other. To me, one of the most interesting—and perhaps the most frightening—aspects is the phenomenon of Internet dating or romance. I have a couple of single friends who have actually gone out with people they originally met over the Internet. One of those friends described the way writing acts as an entry into each other's personality. Her feeling is that you can get to know someone fairly quickly by the way they write and the things they write about—which is a good argument for good writing, right? She feels that it's easier to write to someone than to have an actual conversation—it's not nearly as uncomfortable.

However, as she also admits, it takes a leap of faith to believe that what the other person is saying is true. But what if it's not? Do you think the people involved in this poem are being straight about their real ages? Is the person on the other end making an assumption? What other things can be hidden in a written conversation by simply never being written? What does it mean to "read between the lines"?

The longing?
To connect with others.

1. Write a poem with two voices—kind of like a script—
   that takes place over the Internet. Be sure to give
   your voices great screen names.

2. Before the Internet, we had pen pals. Ask someone
   who is older than you who might have had a pen pal
   and find out what that experience was like. Imagine
   that you have an Internet pen pal. Write a poem about
   him or her. Then write a poem about your online relationship. What is it like? Next, assume that you meet
   face-to-face. What does he or she look like? Are you
   surprised? What happens? Do you continue to corre-
   spond after your meeting?

3. Have you ever longed to be a member of a group of
   people that you watched from a distance? What would
   it take to become part of that group? What might
   keep you out? Write about it.

4. If you were stuck on a desert island and could only
   have three people with you, who would they be? Why
   would you choose them? How would you survive?
   Write a diary of your experiences.

5. Have you ever been in a group in which one person was
   driving everyone else crazy? Write about that person.

Coach's Son

My cousin Mike was a coach's son. His father (my uncle) was always the coach or assistant coach for his Little League baseball teams. Mike was an excellent ballplayer, and my uncle was a great coach. But playing together was not always a happy scenario. My aunt, a very loving woman, was always there to soothe both of them.

The longing?
For comfort and security.

1. When you are stressed out, how do you find comfort? Who do you turn to? What makes you feel safe and relaxed?

2. When you were a baby, did your mom or dad sing a favorite nursery rhyme or song to you? Do you remember it? When you hear it now, how does it make you feel?

3. Many of us do things to please other people, and there is some comfort in doing that; however, we often give up our true heart's desire in the process—things like playing the trombone or acting in the school play.

Write about a time when you gave up something you really wanted to do in order to please someone else.

4. As a little one did you have a favorite toy—maybe a stuffed animal—or a blanket that you loved? Write a poem honoring that object. Hold a retirement party for it. What objects have taken its place, if any?

5. Write a lullaby, a song for falling asleep.

Cheers

I have a friend who can only be described as "driven." That is, she moves through life at a pace faster than the speed of light. She's what is known as a type-A personality—someone who is motivated by achievement. She's an impressive person, a role model for all of us. Regardless of what she sets out to do, she always seems to achieve her goal.

The longing?
For success.

1. Are you, or is someone you know, a type-A personality? If it's you, how do people respond to you? Is it sometimes lonely at the top? If it's a friend, what is it like to always be compared to him or her? Write about it.

2. Write about a project or goal that you really had to work on to achieve. Take us step-by-step through the whole thing. Maybe it was a science project. Maybe it was an audition for the band or choir. Maybe it was winning the attention of someone you had a crush on. Maybe it was earning a privilege. Give a detailed scenario.

3. We've all taken on projects that we didn't finish successfully. Write about one of those.

4. Jealousy creeps up on all of us. Write about a time you felt jealous of someone else. Go ahead, give all the gory details.

5. There are thousands of books about success, particularly in business—most of them are centered around making sales. Take a look at some of these. They usually have "steps to success." Invent a really silly or off-the-wall goal and apply those steps. Make up a funny story about it all.

6. What would make you feel successful? How do you define someone who is successful? Where do you want to be in five years? Ten years? Fifteen years? Write about it.

The Research Paper: A Sestina

A couple of years ago my older son, Jacob, had to write a research paper about polar bears. It reminded me of my own high school and college years, when every spring my English teacher said, "Research time!" I don't ever remember writing about something as neat as polar bears. In fact, I don't remember any of my research papers—that's how interesting they always were! It was fun watching my son browse through the library and then read through the various books he found there. Unlike my own research experiences, Jacob's really seemed to be enjoyable. He was on the trail to discovery!

The longing?
To explore.

1. Next time you have to do a research paper, sit down and really wander around on the page with the information you have. Don't try to force it into an outline or any type of order, just free-write about it—let the words fall where they may. And if your thoughts wander, let them. You'll eventually return to the topic at hand. Allow yourself to make connections through the free flow of ideas.

2. Before you write the actual paper, write a poem about the topic. My poem is written in a very rigid structure called a sestina, which is a French structure made of six stanzas of six lines each (called sestets) and ending with a three-line stanza (or tercet). The key to a sestina falls in the last words of the first six lines. In my poem those words are: (A) bears, (B) circle, (C) ice, (D) clear, (E) straw, (F) sun.

   So, in the first sestet the lines end in ABCDEF. In the next five sestets the pattern goes like this: (2) FAEBDC, (3) CFDABE, (4) ECBFAD, (5) DEACFB, and (6) BDFECA. Then in the tercet, three of the words are buried in the middle and three find themselves on the end. It sounds really complicated, but if you line up the words in their order along the right-hand margin of the page, you can write the lines to meet the words.

   Even though the form is tight, the subject matter has the feeling of wandering all over the place. With this poem, I was exploring the "form" as much as I was exploring the subject matter. I also spent some time thinking about the different uses of the six words that gave the form its structure. Those six words are the last words on the end of the lines of the first stanza. It was a wonderful experience. Go ahead, be brave—write a sestina!

3. Poetry can be about any subject under the sun. Pick an unlikely subject, maybe something from your geometry or biology class, and write a poem. Explore!

4. Write a poem about the experience of doing research— going to the library, choosing a topic, figuring out the thesis, and so forth. Perhaps there was a surprise in the process. Maybe you fell in love in the library? Go for it.

A Circle of Light: A Poem in Five Acts

When I was a student at Texas A&M University, I spent quite a bit of time in the Theater Arts department; I have a minor degree in that field. While I spent more time behind stage, I did have a few roles in plays. The two plays in which I had the biggest parts were Arthur Miller's *The Crucible* and Clark Gesner's *You're a Good Man, Charlie Brown*. What I noticed was that during the run of *The Crucible*, I felt quite serious and almost despondent. During the run of *Charlie Brown*, in which I played the role of Snoopy, I felt lighthearted and joyful. The natures of the plays affected the way I felt. We're also affected by the books we read and the television shows and movies we watch. We can either be uplifted or depressed, depending upon the subject matter.

The best actors know how to separate themselves from their parts. However, it's almost impossible to take on a role and not also take on some of that character's feelings and traits. The tricky part is figuring out where you begin and the character ends. If we consider all the movie stars who have fallen in love on the sets of movies, we can see how difficult this can be.

The longing?
To forgive and be forgiven.

1. Write about a time when you desperately needed forgiveness.

2. Write about a time when you were hurt by someone else. Were you able to forgive him or her? What happened?

3. We are often put in very difficult positions, sometimes through the actions of others, but usually through our own mistakes, and these mistakes always, always affect other people. Maria and Tanner, the young heroes of this poem, have made a huge mistake. Have you ever known someone who has been faced with a major decision, one that involves life or death? Write about it.

4. I chose to write this poem as a "play" with alternating voices. This was my way of honoring Shakespeare, but also a way to emphasize the different "acts" that my characters were performing. More important, the shadows of the original Romeo and Juliet were always present. It gave the poem some heft, and I felt I needed that for such a serious subject. Poetry does not have to follow a particular set of rules, but sometimes rules give the poem substance. Borrow a form from one of the masters and see what happens. Call on Saint Genesius, the patron saint of actors and musicians.

Ms. Dove and Mr. Edgars

Romance in the workplace is always tricky, and in schools it's especially important for teachers to keep their professional and private lives separate. Still, think about how hard it would be to truly care about another person and not be allowed to exhibit that caring.

Also, consider Valentine's Day, weddings, romance novels, sweetheart bracelets—all the ways we celebrate romantic love. We're surrounded by it. And how wonderful when it happens to us! Despite its wonder, romance often comes with a price. But would we give it up? Nah!

The longing?
For romance.

1. Write a poem about a secret love, one that couldn't be shared without serious consequences.

2. Poetry has been the domain of love for centuries. Write a bunch of really sappy love poems. Make valentines out of them.

3. A favorite form for love poems is the sonnet, and no one did them better than Shakespeare. But instead of

following the traditional Italian form of the day, he made up his own. The Italian (or Petrarchan) sonnet has an octave (eight lines) followed by a sestet (six lines), and the rhymes go like this: ABBAABBA for the octave, and CDECDE, CDCCDC, or CDEDCE for the sestet.

Shakespeare, craftsman that he was, came up with three quatrains (four lines) and a final couplet (two lines), and his typical rhyme schemes were like this: ABAB CDCD EFEF GG.

The kicker in the sonnet is that it usually sets up an argument in the first several lines and then resolves the argument in the final sestet or couplet. Critics say that the sonnet is the quintessential love poem, the highest form of the poetic craft. Try writing both an Italian and a Shakespearean sonnet.

The Yearbook Photographer

My husband worked as a photographer for a number of years. Once in a while I accompanied him to a wedding. After the formal pictures were taken, he would attend the reception, where he became almost invisible, snapping photos of the guests. Yearbook photographers are the same way, slipping through the crowd, looking for the right shots, the perfect moments.

The longing?
To disappear.

1. Have you ever been in a situation in which you needed to be invisible in order to get the job done? In other words, has there ever been a time in your life when you needed to be "behind the scenes"? Did you enjoy it? Write about it.

2. List all the people you know whom you think of as creative: the girl who always gets the lead in the school play, the girl who makes beaded jewelry, the boy who wins the art contest, the guys who play together in a band, the old woman who makes hats, the man who carves Civil War figurines out of pecan shells. Choose

one and describe him or her, then describe what the person does. Be specific.

3. How often do you spend time by yourself? What do you particularly enjoy doing when you are alone? What if you were required to spend a whole weekend by yourself? What would you do to fill up the time?

4. Next time you go to an event—a concert, a basketball game, a movie—pay attention to the folks we usually don't see: the ushers, referees, ticket takers, janitors, valet parking attendants. Write a poem about one of them.

Dumpling

One of my best friends was the victim of abuse at the hands of her stepfather. Today she is a powerful and successful businesswoman, but the old scars of that abuse remain with her. Even those of us who have had the good fortune to grow up in a loving and respectful family have had moments in our lives which were extremely frightening or painful. No one is totally exempt. Even those whose lives seem the most charmed often have skeletons in their closets—an alcoholic parent, a terrible secret, a traumatic event. The way we cope differs from person to person. I choose to tell stories, write poems.

The longing?
To escape.

1. Many of us have things from which we'd like to escape. For some people, these are serious: abuse, trauma, illness, addiction. Even if nothing like these have ever happened to you, it may have happened to someone you know. Write a poem in which your main character manages to overcome a serious situation.

2. Ask your parents or grandparents about a time when they escaped from something, then write a poem

about their experiences. Be sure to include all the details.

3. Ask your parents or grandparents about a time when they had to fight for something. Write about that too.

4. Have you ever been in a situation in which you had to choose between fighting and fleeing? If not, make up a scene. Give it two endings and call one scenario "fight" and the other "flight."

5. History is full of daring rescues and fantastic escapes. The Underground Railroad gave rise to many rescues and escapes. Look through your history book and find other instances of one or the other. Write a poem as if you were participating.

6. Celebrities often have a penchant for telling all. That is, they aren't always shy about airing out their pasts, even if it means revealing stories of abuse or incest or neglect. We usually admire them, seeing them as survivors. Find a famous person who was a victim and write a poem about him or her. Try writing a letter poem, a poem that's actually addressed to someone. Naomi Shihab Nye created a wonderful example of a letter poem in "A Valentine for Ernest Mann."

7. Many brilliant artists, athletes, and scientists led tormented childhoods. One of the most puzzling questions for psychiatrists is how these people find the strength to move beyond their troubled pasts and rise to the top. They are truly role models. Do some research. Find some of these folks and write about them. See if you can figure out why they made it.

Notes Passed Back and Forth in U.S. History Class, Seventh Period

When I was in school my friends and I passed notes to each other all the time, usually right under the noses of our teachers. And, oh, how I lived for the notes from my sweetheart, a handsome fellow named Brett. Unfolding the ruled notebook paper in the middle of my government class made my heart race. Knowing that passing notes was against the rules made it all the more wonderful. Kinda risky. Kinda thrilling. Try it and then blame it on me.

The longing?
To play.

1. I'll bet that the Japanese masters who created haiku would love the idea of passing notes written in that form. After all, haiku came into being when several great poets decided to hold contests to see who could write the best first line. Of course, as with any contest, rules had to be made—thus, the 5/7/5 rule of syllables. Get together with a friend and try writing haiku notes

back and forth. You might be surprised by what you think up to say.

2. Hold a limerick contest. A limerick is a five-line rhyming poem in which lines 1, 2, and 5 end in one rhyme, and lines 3 and 4 end in another. Many limericks are downright ribald, making the crustiest sailor blush. Ogden Nash was the king of limericists. Take a look at some of his limericks and then write your own.

3. Write a whole poem using nothing but puns.

4. Do you know what a palindrome is? It's a word or line that is spelled the same way backward and forward, like "Otto" and "star rats" and "too hot to hoot." See if you can write a four-line poem using only palindromes.

5. Just enjoy writing for a change!

The Driver's License

I remember the day(s) I took my driving test. I failed it the first time, but that's all I recall about that one. However, the second time around could've happened yesterday. I can still see the officer, his long legs crunched up because I had to have the seat so close to the steering wheel. (I'm not very tall.) I can still hear his pen scratching on that brown clipboard. I can still see him tearing off the form he had filled out, the one I carried inside to the Department of Transportation office, where the lady at the desk took my picture and charged me three dollars. What a day! I had an overwhelming feeling of success.

The longing?
For power.

1. Do you have your driver's license? Write a poem about your driving test. What was the part that was most bedeviling? What part was easiest?

2. What would you do if you were in a position of power? What if you could be boss, principal, parent, or president? How would you run things?

3. Examine the word *power.* Make a list of the many forms it takes: Black Power, PowerAde, word power, "we've got the power." Do any of them fit into your life? Write about them.

4. Think about a warning or an old saying someone has repeated to you all your life, then write a poem using that warning. Does using it make you feel powerful? As if taking it and making it your own took some of the heat out of it—or put some heat into it?

5. Have you recently passed a test—not just a driving test, but any test? The SAT? An English final? A blood test? A drug screen? A physical exam? How did it make you feel? Write about it.

6. Can you think of other objects that represent power? What are they? Make a list.

Apply Yourself!

As a rather goal-oriented person, I have often found myself caught up in work or a project, in deadlines and obligations. It's easy to do in our fast-paced and competitive society. I think students these days are bombarded. You need to make high scores on exams, you have to do well in your classes, you need to be involved. You need to look good on paper. In the process, we lose some things, like a sense of wonder, the joy of doing a job well, the pleasure in just having a soft drink with someone you like, the peacefulness of a long walk. Sometimes in the hurly-burly of life, we miss out on *life*.

The longing?
To find out what matters, to see what is true.

1. Make a list of things that really matter to you. Of course, that list may include good grades and high test scores. That's fine. What else matters?

2. This poem is called a litany because most of the lines start with the same phrase or words. We get litanies from liturgical or sacred texts. Listen to a chant and you'll hear certain lines over and over. It's no real sur-

prise that a litany can also be a prayer, a search for what matters. Choose a phrase and try your own. Here are some examples:

Thank you . . .
Try this . . .
Because . . .
Tomorrow I will . . .
This is the . . .
When you said . . .
I remember . . .
Do you recall . . .
Let us sing . . .

3. Sometimes what we think is important turns out not to be important at all. Has that ever happened to you? Maybe you begged your parents to let you go somewhere—a party, a dance—and it turned out not to be all it was cracked up to be. Maybe you would have been happier staying at home with your parents and watching a good movie. Learning what is true is not often easy. Write about finding out something true the hard way.

What He Took with Him

Growing up is often difficult, and there are times when "getting out on our own" just can't happen soon enough. Now that my sons are growing older and preparing to leave, I'm trying hard, as their mom, to let them go. One morning while I was writing, I started thinking about one of them just walking out the door and how that would feel for both of us.

The longing?
For freedom.

1. What would happen if someone you knew ran away? What would he or she take along?

2. If you had to leave your home and could only take what you could carry, what would you take?

3. Being completely free comes with all kinds of responsibilities. Make a list of the things you would be responsible for if you were completely independent. Take an inventory. How much money would you need in order to live on your own?

4. If you could take off and go anywhere you wanted, where would you go? Who would you take with you? What would you do once you got there? Who would you miss? Who would miss you?

5. If you could give up something that is dragging you down, what would it be? How would you get it off your back?

6. Have you ever had a pet that ran away or got stolen? What was that like? How did you feel? Write about it.

The Science Fair

When my husband and I lived in Iowa, we met a colleague who loved to watch birds. His enthusiasm was contagious, and soon we began to watch them, too. It's the kind of activity that reminds us to be alert, to pay attention, to be surprised. It's a wonderful way to feel connected to nature.

Nature reminds us that we are all essential, that we all have a role to play here on Earth. It also reminds us of the awesome presence of creation. Some call that presence God, some call it spirit, some don't name it at all—we simply feel and know the wonder of life.

The longing?
To be a part of something larger than ourselves.

1. Allow yourself some time to really observe your neighborhood. Buy a notebook and call it a field notebook. List the plants and trees, the wildflowers and birds that are right in your own vicinity. I was once told that the best thing a writer could do was learn the names of plants and animals because they make your writing feel substantial. It's true. Try writing a list poem, similar to this one, of the wildflowers along the road.

2. Write a list poem of places where you like to be or go. Write brief descriptions of them.

3. Choose a particular animal, perhaps a dog, and then make a list of all the breeds you can think of. Write a poem using as many of those names as possible. Call it "Dog Show." You can do the same thing with any species. Have fun.

4. Often, writing about nature gives us a sense of gratitude. Write a poem about the things you are grateful for.

5. Make an alphabet of different kinds of animals—a cat alphabet, a bird alphabet, a horse alphabet. Play with the language of animals.

6. Biology, environment, and botany classes are rich resources for poems about nature. If you are enrolled in one of these, or if you have already taken one, dig out your textbook and use some of those fancy vocabulary words to make a poem. Make several poems.

7. Go to the library and find some of those wonderful nature magazines—*National Geographic, Defenders, Audubon*. Pick an article to use as the basis for a poem. Look at the poetry of Edward Abbey *(Earth Apples)* for an interesting example of nature poetry. Make your own collection of nature poems.

The Twirling Queen of Dogwood, Texas

I've always been intrigued by baton twirlers. How in the world do they get their fingers to go so fast? How do they catch those things without chopping off their noses? In fact, I'm always in awe of anyone who does something extremely well. I guess we all are, especially when that person exudes passion about what he or she is doing.

One of the most difficult things for us is to discover what we are supposed to do with our lives. As a young adult I worked in a restaurant. The manager, whose name was Skip, was a gifted leader. He did a great job of inspiring his workers, and he was very efficient. The company loved him and the way he went about doing his job. However, he was extremely unhappy. Why? Because what he really wanted to do was teach school. However, both of his parents were schoolteachers, and for some reason they did not want Skip to follow in their footsteps. Out of deference to them, he chose a different occupation. But what a price he paid!

The longing?
To be true to one's own heart.

1. What are you passionate about? What would you be willing to give up in order to make your dreams come true? Write a letter to your heart. What does it say?

2. Have you ever met or heard of someone who seemed to have it all and then turned away from it? Write about him or her.

3. What other activities besides baton twirling are out of the norm? Spinning yo-yos? Performing contortions? Sword swallowing? Belly dancing? Motorcycle jumping? Write a poem about someone who is really good at one of these. Do some research on what you have to do in order to become good at it. Interview people who do something special and see what inspired them.

4. Sometimes inspiration happens by accident. Maybe you meet someone who tells you about an opportunity; or maybe you read about it while you are waiting for a haircut. Be on the alert for "happy accidents." Then write about them.

5. Throughout history, people have heard voices or spirits. Joan of Arc is a great example of someone who paid attention to those callings; there are others. Write a poem to someone who was led by a higher power, someone who listened.

Night Mares

I love to play with words, especially when they can have such different meanings. Usually the term *nightmares* makes me think of bad dreams. But in this case, I've tried to turn something scary into something wondrous and appealing. I also used to imagine that small creatures lived underneath my bed and came out at night. Horses were always my favorite. By connecting the memory of these underbed imaginings to the reality of my grandmother, I hope the poem has a reassuring rather than a frightening tone. At the same time, I hope the fantasy remains.

The longing?
To dream.

1. Begin a poem with "Remember when . . ." and keep going.

2. Begin a poem with "What if . . ." and keep going.

3. All of us have dreams, either comforting or scary. By writing about the scary ones, we can often make them less frightening. By writing about the good ones,

we can relish the present and the future. Write about them all.

4. Write about a moment when you were very still. What did you notice about the stillness? Was your imagination able to take flight? Why not find a quiet moment and set it free?

5. Make a list of some of the things you did when you were younger. Did you ever pretend you were someone else? A movie star? A knight in shining armor? A princess in a tower? Write about those times.

6. What do you dream for yourself? Make a list.

Some Helpful Books on Writing Poetry (and anything else, but mainly poetry)

Appelt, Kathi. *Just People & Paper/Pen/Poem: A Young Writer's Way to Begin.* Spring, TX: Absey & Co., 1997.

Corn, Alfred. *The Poem's Heartbeat: A Manual of Prosody.* Brownsville, OR: Story Line Press, 1997.

Dunning, Stephen, and William Stafford. *Getting the Knack: 20 Poetry Writing Exercises.* Urbana, IL: National Council of Teachers of English, 1992.

Fox, John. *Finding What You Didn't Lose: Expressing Your Truth and Creativity Through Poem-Making.* New York: Jeremy P. Tarcher/ G. P. Putnam's Sons, 1995.

Fox, John. *Poetic Medicine: The Healing Art of Poem-Making.* New York: Jeremy P. Tarcher/G. P. Putnam's Sons, 1997.

Goldberg, Natalie. *Writing Down the Bones: Freeing the Writer Within.* Boston: Shambhala Publications, 1986.

Heard, Georgia. *Writing Toward Home: Tales and Lessons to Find Your Way.* Portsmouth, NH: Heinemann, 1995.

Joselow, Beth Baruch. *Writing Without the Muse: 60 Beginning Exercises for the Creative Writer.* Brownsville, OR: Story Line press, 1999.

Kirby, David. *Writing Poetry: Where Poems Come From and How to Write Them.* Boston: The Writer, Inc., 1989.

Kowit, Steve. *In the Palm of Your Hand: The Poet's Portable Workshop.* Gardiner, ME: Tilbury House, 1995.

Lamott, Anne. *Bird by Bird: Some Instruments on Writing and Life.* New York: Pantheon, 1994.

Lehman, David. *The Daily Mirror: A Journal in Poetry.* New York: Scribner/Simon & Schuster, 2000.

Livingston, Myra Cohn. *Poem-Making: Ways to Begin Writing Poetry.* New York: HarperCollins, 1991.

Lyon, George Ella. *Where I'm From: Where Poems Come From.* Spring, TX: Absey & Co., 1999.

Oliver, Mary. *A Poetry Handbook.* New York: Harcourt Brace, Inc., 1994.

Padgett, Ron, ed. *Handbook of Poetic Forms.* New York: Teachers & Writers, 1987.

Stafford, William. *Writing the Australian Crawl: Views on the Writer's Vocation.* Ann Arbor: University of Michigan Press, 1978.

Stafford, William. *You Must Revise Your Life.* Ann Arbor: University of Michigan Press, 1986.

Wooldridge, Susan Goldsmith. *Poemcrazy: Freeing Your Life with Words.* New York: Clarkson Potter, 1996.

CPSIA information can be obtained at www.ICGtesting.com
Printed in the USA
LVOW090402190412

278258LV00001B/50/P

9 780805 075960